FROM:

DON CARTER

TO:

SEND IT!

Roaring Brook Press
Brookfield, Connecticut

FRAGILE

Monday

Wrap it. Tape it.

Address it.

Send it.

Truck it.

Lift it.

Balance it.

Don't drop it!

Tuesday

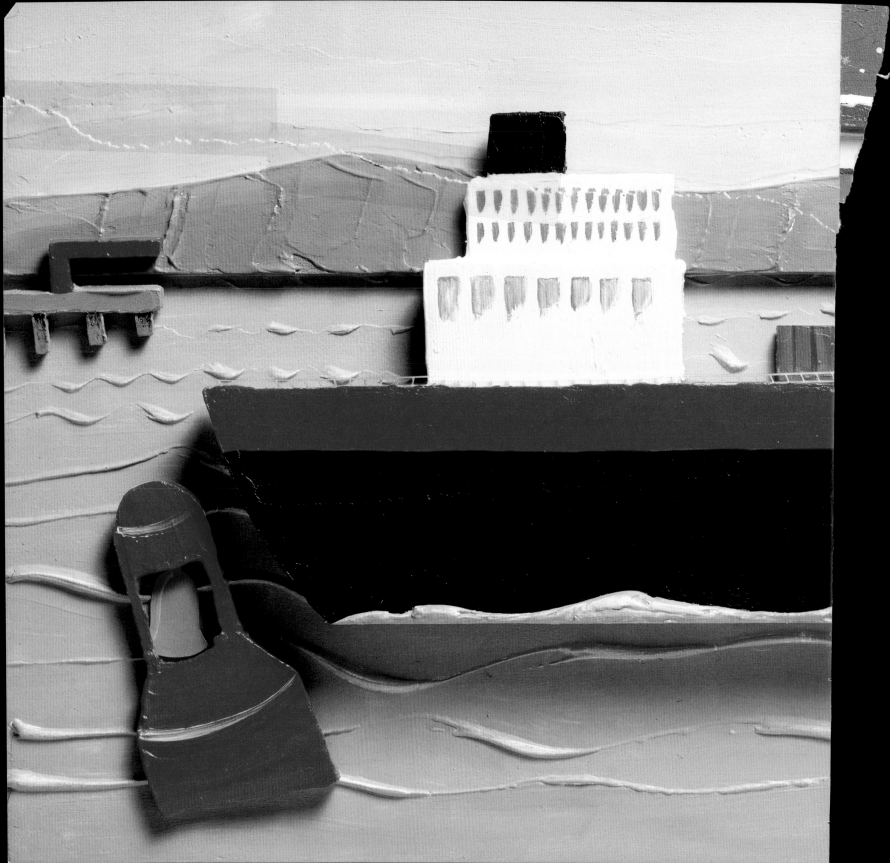

Wednesday

Unload it.

Push it.

Careful
with it. . . .

Move it.

Thursday

Stack it.   Don't lose it.

Choo-choo it.

Saturday

Drive it.   Carry it.

Open it.

Say thank you for it!

Copyright © 2003 by Don Carter. Published by Roaring Brook Press, A Division of The
Millbrook Press, 2 Old New Milford Road, Brookfield, Connecticut 06804. All rights reserved.

Library of Congress Cataloging-in-Publication Data
Carter, Don, 1958—
Send it / Don Carter.—1st ed.
    p. cm.
Summary: Simple text and illustrations describe a package as it makes its way across country,
from the time it is wrapped and addressed until it is delivered and opened.
[1. Postal service—Fiction.] I. Title.
PZ7.C2432Se 2003   [E]—dc22   2003016633

ISBN 0-7613-1578-0 (trade) 10 9 8 7 6 5 4 3 2 1
ISBN 0-7613-2573-5 (library binding) 10 9 8 7 6 5 4 3 2 1
Book design by Tania Garcia   Printed in the United States of America   First edition

For my big brother, Dave